# Fowl Tales

## by Stan Perkins

*Taken for granted, but they were like money in the bank.*

**Broadblade Press**

Swartz Creek, Michigan
48473-8570

Copyright by Stan Perkins 2002

All rights reserved. No part of this publication may be reproduced or utilized in any form or means electrical or mechanically including photocopying, recording, information storage or retrieval systems, without written permission from the publisher.

Broadblade Press
11314 Miller Road
Swartz Creek Michigan 48473-8590

Any and all inquiries must be addressed to Broadblade Press

Unless otherwise indicated, all photographs are from the author's collection and neighbors with their permission.

ISBN: 0-9713893-0-6

Printed in the United States of America by
McNaughton & Gunn

# Acknowledgements

Peggy Abrams
Donald Chapman
Mildred Crapser-Smith
Marguerite Donal
Flint Public Library
Genesee District Library
Myrtie Hier
Edmon Holloway
Erin Sims Howarth
Frances Jewel

Mark Kulig
Lucinda Long
Loleta Potter
Linda Purdy
Susan Rodriguez
Thomas Rohrer
George Ryva
Richard and Ronda Woods
United States Department of Agriculture

And to all those who have assisted by giving encouragement and support to preserving pioneer humor, educational background, folklore, and historical records for future generations, Thank you.

*A fine Wild Turkey brood foraging under strict parental supervision behind a predator repelling fence.*

# Illustrations

| Illustration | Page |
|---|---|
| The Boss | cover |
| White Leghorn Family | i |
| Wild Turkeys with Brood | iii |
| Chinese Ring-Necked Cock Pheasant in corn | 2 |
| Ancient Poultry House | 3 |
| An Egg is Laid | 4 |
| Problem Solvers | 5 |
| White Wyandottes | 6 |
| Family Sized Coop | 8 |
| Fighting Cocks | 9 |
| Relaxing Image | 10 |
| Security | 11 |
| A Brooder House | 14 |
| Let's put it back in Service | 15 |
| Flabbergasted Mother Hen | 16 |
| Beautiful Bird | 18 |
| Contentment | 19 |
| Attractive Chicken Coops | 20 |
| New Hampshires | 20 |
| Pair of Orpingtons | 21 |
| Plymouth White Rocks | 22 |
| Flock of Rhode Island Reds and Box Social Owners | 23 |
| Afraid of Water | 26 |
| Motherless Young Fowl | 27 |
| Photos of Ducks and Geese | 29 |

| Illustration | Page |
|---|---|
| Protection | 30 |
| Enjoyable Pets | 32 |
| Our Chicken Plant | 34 |
| Rhode Island Red Escapees | 38 |
| Where do we find a Rooster | 39 |
| The Culprit | 43 |
| Buff Orpingtons | 48 |
| No! Is Not the Answer | 50 |
| Door Open for Early Crowers | 52 |
| Young Perk Shelling Corn for his Buddies | 53 |
| An Ideal Family Plant | 57 |
| The Poultry Business | 62 |
| A Money Maker Size | 65 |
| Catch-all Building | 66 |
| Low Cholesterol | 68 |
| Internal View of Working System | 69 |
| Integrated Egg Production Unit | 70 |
| What a Pile of Eggs | 71 |
| Mass Production | 72 |
| Flooded Out: Is It Volume or Quantity? | 74 |
| Plymouth Rock: An Ideal Dinner | 75 |
| The Beautiful Chick, Again | 78 |

# Contents
# Off the Roost

|  |  |  |
|---|---|---|
|  | Prologue | 1 |
| Chapter 1 | Early Predicaments | 7 |
| Chapter 2 | Poultry Pets | 13 |
| Chapter 3 | The Process | 17 |
| Chapter 4 | Potpourri of Ducks and Geese | 25 |
| Chapter 5 | Chicken Roundup | 35 |
| Chapter 6 | Sticky Stuff | 41 |
| Chapter 7 | Poultry Poachers and Thieves | 51 |
| Chapter 8 | Granny's Luscious Meals | 63 |

## Other Books written and/or collaborated by Stan Perkins:

*Arvilla and the Tattler Tree*

*Axe Thrower of the Tittabawassee*

*The Blue-Eyed Chippewa*

*Genessee County Fair Since 1850*

*Itinerant Auctioneering*

*The House Coveted*

*Lore of Wolverine Country*

*No Ordinary Crime*

*Oh! For the Life of a Country Girl*

*Perk's Path*

*Spooky Barns*

*Tina*

*Too Many People*

*We're From Duffield*

# Prologue

*Fowl Tales* is an introduction to an essential segment of folklore we define as food. Specifically, the quality of food.

Napoleon Bonaparte was quoted as saying, "Armies travel on their stomachs." The same is true of pioneers settling a new land. When food became scarce, progress dwindled, then ceased. Early Americans depended on wild game following the pattern set by their predecessors, the Native Indians. The quality of this nourishment was excellent for energy and succulent, too.

When our ancestors took up and cleared the land for agriculture, this abundance of nature's supply of wild game diminished. The demand for quality foods remained while quantity decreased.

Domesticated fowl and animals arose and replaced nature's gift of nourishment. The gap was closed by improved specimens. Barnyard poultry quickly became the most popular food source and remains so to this day. However, with all things good, there must be recompensation by way of equalization. Demand requires a change in methods as demonstrated in the obsolete chicken coop.

This publication continues a program to preserve folklore of yesterday. Poultry is a seldom recognized commodity. It is largely ignored by the citizenry. When combined with a multitude of associated food products it becomes our heritage. Heritage has been the predictable weathervane of humanity for thousands of years and will continue into the unforeseen future.

The particular subject matter being used in this publication of folklore has to do entirely with birds, or *aves*. The species is specifically domestic poultry with varieties ranging the field from chickens, ducks, geese, turkeys, to squab, quail, pheasant, partridge, and even prairie hens. This study is humorous, entertaining, and educational. Fowl have always been treasured, even back in prehistoric times, for their eggs, meat and feathers. They have been commonplace, completely overlooked, and taken for granted.

Records are vague. By boiling down facts as presented from several sources the bird we call a chicken was dispersed about the planet from Southeastern Asia. He was wild and red. Found in the jungles of India and named scientifically "Gallus Gallus," his appearance was more like a fighting cock than our present domesticated fowl.

My personal choice of foods is a Chinese, ring-necked cock pheasant taken from our own cornfield. He never went hungry a day in his life, and was hatched by his mother the previous spring in the adjoining fence row. Note the image in the cornstalks below.

**Nature's Food**

courtesy of The Flint Public Library

*An old style henhouse built a century ago with the second set of windows offset in the roof to allow more sunshine in on those cold clear winter days. It fooled the hens into thinking it was spring so they would lay earlier.*

The chicken was the first domestic fowl. It was recorded in ancient Chinese drawings and writings before 1400 B.C. Babylonian carvings depicted fowl in 600 B.C. Greek writers used them as illustrations by 400 B.C. Romans considered chickens sacred. A rooster was used as an example of courage and stability.

The French Republic later adopted the Cock as their national symbol. An aggressive rooster was the emblem of our Democratic Party from 1842 until 1874. Today chicken is the most important class of domestic poultry and is dispersed all over this planet Earth. For centuries, poultry raising has been an essential portion of agriculture and our food supply. In size and shape all fowl have great diversity. They have supported a host of predators and *Homo sapiens* to boot.

The giant twelve-pound Brahma Cock, for example, has a miniature counterpart, the Banty, weighing only twenty ounces. Some fowl are bred for egg production with some Leghorn Hibreds producing as many as two hundred fifty eggs per season. Others are raised strictly for meat production and are marketed at specific weights in response to special demand as fryers or roasters. A few breeds are raised exclusively for their feathers to

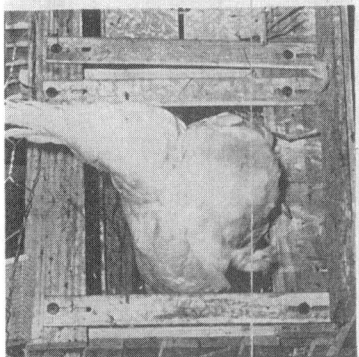

courtesy of The Flint Public Library

*In this sequence of images an egg is laid. It is ready to be consumed for breakfast—as fresh as they come. It can also be used in cooking or, if fertile, incubated for twenty-one days to produce a fuzzy chick. The egg comes first?*

decorate hats, dresses, and cloaks. The demand and resulting market is unlimited.

The cocks are polyamous. The high fecundity of this species is important because both the eggs and meat are high protein foods.

At this writing, hoof and mouth disease, together with a virus called mad cow disease, are serious threats to our red meat supply. Let's hope they are controlled, but if not, where would we go for our protein? To poultry products, not beans.

Writers are supposed to do their best work when intensely acquainted with the subject. I meet that qualification, and feel like a productive hen that has just laid an egg. She boasts of her ability by cackling for all to hear, "Look, Oh, look! Look what I did, look what I did."

The value of poultry exports has been billions of dollars per year so economically they have helped to keep our balance of payments to within striking distance of correction.

The style of this bit of folklore writing is often lost between the lines because the real meanings were disguised by the clucks of a setting hen.

*Problem solvers—always available when needed.*

Chicks are hatched from fertile eggs. They are well prepared for life, not naked, but covered with a heavy down and prepared to live for several days on the egg yolk retained in their abdomen.

As a leading commercial enterprise, poultry did not materialize until the twentieth century. Then it was removed from the individual farm family and became big business. This is when we lost much of the Ohs! and Ahs! That will be discussed later. Invention abruptly brought the tasty home products to a halt. Efficient incubators, mass brooding equipment plus mass breeding and chemical feeds left the individual small operator standing beside his country road with his mouth open and his poultry coop empty.

At this point you are asking, "What does this have to do with my personal well-being and about tossing valuable folklore to the winds, thus losing it forever?" The answer is a tough one. It's called progress.

No argument, poultry and wild game have provided more tasty, quality protein to our diet than any other type of nourishment. It has been the staff of life. Not bread. Often the specter of starvation was driven from the doors of our ancestors' cabins by meat and eggs produced by a small flock of chickens, usually less than a dozen. What more could one ask for? Within the echelon of foods, poultry and its products remains near the top.

*A White Wyandotte cock and pullet*

# Chapter One
# Early Predicaments

My first encounter with poultry was not good. It included only two people, my paternal grandmother and myself. A third person cannot be held responsible. My maternal grandfather, a hardware merchant in a small town, was not accountable for my actions even though he set it up. As a five-year-old I was just crazy to be around his store. Hardwares remain my favorite stores today.

My preferred items he stocked were nails. Next came hammers; I could have been an apprentice carpenter early.

To keep me amused and out of trouble he would let me play around his nail bins. I could not do anything with those big nails he called railroad spikes, but I liked the box sixes that had oversized head. I couldn't miss them with my hammer and hit my finger. I got into a little trouble when I drove a few nails into a new wood chicken crate and a back window sill in his store.

Grandpa Lee retarded my destructive habit by bringing two blocks of wood into his back room. He provided a short one for me to sit on and another longer one he stood on end and let me pound nails into it. That worked out fine. Soon someone routed me from my ecstasy by calling out, "Come on, young man, the buggy is waiting."

*A typical family laying house that has a capacity of forty hens. Note the customary rhubarb at the corner. Poultry and this pie plant thrive as bedfellows. The door here is nailed open.*

I rushed off to go home but not without my hammer and a supply of nails. Once home there were lots of things to nail. I went across the road to the farm and everything I came to needed a few nails.

While back home eating super there came a furious pounding at our kitchen door. It was my paternal grandmother, Henrietta. She couldn't get the henhouse door open and she needed some eggs for supper.

"Why did you nail it shut?" she cried, addressing my father. Poor fellow, he knew not what she was raving about.

"The chicken coop door is nailed shut."

All eyes turned toward me. I had nearly caused a family riot!

"Why did you do that?" Dad asked.

"I didn't think it should be swinging back and forth in the wind all day."

To quiet Grandmother's concerns, I was ordered to bed with no more supper. Luck was with me. No razor strap.

When he returned from the family chicken coop, I heard him

tell mother that that door should have been closed by the last person to use it. Who? Grandmother Henrietta.

One of my first recollections of chickens was when my mother gave me the egg basket and sent me out to the henhouse to gather and fetch her a few eggs. Something was in the oven of the kitchen range and she could not leave. She always had a couple of hungry hired farm hands to feed in addition to our own family.

Off I trudged. Opening the coop door I spied a large Barred Rock hen on the first nest. I noticed she was covering a pile of luscious brown eggs. I tried to scare her off the nest, but she wouldn't budge and vigorously pecked my little hand. As I tried to take some of her eggs she did not have the slightest idea of leaving her treasure for me to rob. As a youngster, when meeting up with opposition my temper flared. I grabbed her by the neck and tossed her on the henhouse dirt floor. Did she raise a rumpus. Wow! Even tried to fly up against my short legs and spur me like a rooster when fighting another cock. My mother, Rubena, had given me a job. She was my all, my idol. Having no intention of returning without eggs, I scooped the whole nest full of eggs into my basket and took off on a run for the house.

courtesy of U.S.D.A.

*When I was a lad our hired hands were always bragging about their fighting cocks. Before I attended school, this was the source of all my information. Left to right, these are Black Game Cock, Modern Fighter, Sumatra Cock, Old English Game Cock. These were considered valuable. Often more than a month's wages would be bet on one cock fight.*

"Set them over there on the wood box, I don't need

them just yet. My, Stanley! You came back in a hurry."

I did as told and went back outdoors to play with my new pup, Rex. We were lollygagging about the backyard chasing barn cats up trees when a terrible yell came out to us from the kitchen screen door. It was my mother calling for me to come hither. The yell had been bloodcurdling. Now her speaking voice was tense and forebode trouble for me. Who else? There was nobody about except Rex and me. I approached that kitchen door cautiously and slowly. She ordered curtly, "Stanley, come here. Take these eggs back to the henhouse and put them back where you found them, quickly."

I took off on a run, following her orders. While rounding the woodpile I stubbed my toe and away flew the eggs, busting them all. A pile of split wood was no place to be losing a basket of eggs. This was double trouble. As I picked up I was a mess. Looking about at the broken eggs, it was plain to see that they all contained baby chicks well on the way to hatching.

I had no choice but to go back to the kitchen in my wet, egg-dripping clothes. I opened the door carefully, and there sat my mother, crying. This caused me to sob as well. She had broken one of those eggs into her cake batter. It was tragic. When dad and his hired hands arrived, I was in for the licking of my young life, but immediately Mother broke out in a laugh. She came to me and gave me a big bear hug followed by a smacker that had always previously been reserved for only when I did something good. For a moment I was completely confused.

*Pride of ownership and nature's scenic beauty are combined here in this private pond. The view of this wildfowl group is accented by a pair of swans in the foreground. They could all be called pets until they fly away to a warmer clime after the leaves fall.*

*Source of a good bread and butter income.*

She pitched the bowl of cake batter out the back door. It was licked up by Rex and the barn cats. Next, Mother took a foot tub of warm water from the range reservoir, took my clothes off and gave me a bath.

There was no cake for supper but she told the men why. I listened. The egg she broke for her cake contained a nearly fully developed chick almost ready to hatch. They all had a big laugh, except me. My mother, Ruby, as most people called her, was the greatest person in my life.

There were so many problems that surfaced during a twenty-four hour day for a woman in the country that this angel food cake was soon forgotten except by Rex. He liked it. One of the many problems for farm women was pinfeathers. Twice in a chicken's life, pinfeathers are bad. Pinfeathers occur before the chickens reach maturity and during molting, a period when they shed the old and grow new feathers.

The in-laws had been invited for supper to show off our new power washing machine, the great drudgery and back saver. There was no refrigeration, no way to keep fresh meat for over a few hours. There was only one answer, chicken.

Company can come regardless of these natural changes in a fowl's life. A large chicken dinner is a necessity. Many of the cook's efforts do not correspond with the chicken's schedule. About half the time pinfeathers are in season, regardless of when a chicken must be taken to the chopping block.

Nobody seemed to skin a chicken to remove pinfeathers completely. It had to be intact to retain the natural fat and juices that brought out the distinctive flavor of a barnyard chicken, a flavor that has been lost. As previously mentioned, connoisseurs of good food will never know the tang of fried, roasted barnyard chicken. If a cook gets stuck with a chicken carcass peppered with slugs of embryo feathers, unpresentable to guests, there is no choice. They must be removed individually. It takes at least an hour to do a good job so the bird will not be damaged and the table presentation will be improved. It is a chore often performed by an unsung hero, a country cook. This chore is endured quietly, alone with her bird. A bit of toil tolerated without comment.

It is equal to the repair work of sewing on buttons, mending rips and untwisting overall shoulder straps, untangling a mess often found in wet half-washed clothing around the agitator of an early power washing machine.

No complaint, no comment. The dinner appears to have gone off without a hitch. Out of respect we should place extra flowers on the resting places of these Great Grannies whom many of us never knew. Nobody was ever better at smoothing out the rough spots. They happened every day in country living.

## Chapter Two
# Poultry Pets

Seldom is it impossible to lift a hand to record an incident of this wonderful life that has been given so freely to me. It is the result of the greatest education ever conceived on our planet: the one room country school.

One day each year, preferably in the spring, was designated "Pet Day." Each student was supposed to bring a pet to school that day. Our teacher was Miss Roberta Fuller. If a student cooperated he received an A, if he did not show with a pet his mark for the day was an E or failure. It was good experience for students to show and tell before other people besides classmates.

The teacher had special responsibilities. Many parents came, as well as others in the community, even those with no children. At noon it turned into a community potluck. It was held outdoors if the weather cooperated. If not, most pets were put in the woodshed. A sumptuous meal would be held inside the school for the students and our guests.

The list of pets was varied all the way from a horse to a butterfly. My pet, as you would suspect, was a chicken less than a month out of confinement. An escapee from the shell. Dode, as I called him, went to the pet show in the pocket of my everyday sweater. The pocket had a hole in it out of which I stuck his curious head. We got started down Maple Avenue to our Ryno School, a journey of one and a half miles. He settled down during the walk and let me button down the flap on my pocket.

*A brooder house where young fowl are started when purchased from a hatchery. No mother hens are allowed or needed. This size was for about a hundred chicks.*

Before I got to school he was asleep. It came my turn in the show. I had not fed Dode since morning so he was good and hungry. In my other pocket I brought along a handful of wheat. He also liked grass and insects but was sick and tired of chick starter mash that would stick in his throat. Whole kernels of wheat were his bag. I had Dode perform for my schoolmates and spectators by making him work to get his feed. I used large books from a set of old encyclopedias, the only reference books the school had in its sparse library. I used the teacher's desk as a stage—much to her chagrin. I built a pile of those books so they resembled a chicken stairway with inducement of a few kernels. I wanted to see how far Dode would continue climbing and risk his neck for feed.

Spectators were cheering him on. A couple of men bet each other that he would not make the sixth step. Dode had performed other tricks for me to get kernels. I built a dark tunnel from the same books and hid the wheat in the unseen corners of a maze. He had a good memory. Not all his brains were in his crop, I told the onlookers. A few were in his head. Before sitting down and placing Dode in a waste basket for safe keeping, I was challenged by a lady sitting at a school desk in the back of the room. It was Mrs. Joe Ringlein.

"Perkins, your pet is not a male. You're going to have to change his name. Change it from your masculine Dode to Dodie. That pet of yours is going to be a pullet shortly, then later on an old hen stealing her nest, laying eggs, then showing up with a hatch of fuzzy little ones to prove to you what she can really do. This pullet you have trained well thinks you're her mother hen."

Mrs. Ringlein knew her chickens. She was a great country cook with a table full to plan and prepare food for three times each day.

*A typical, lonesome, unused family chicken coop. Let's put it back into service. Flowers always grow profusely about an unused crop, especially those great hollyhocks.*

## A Poultry Problem

*A White Rock Setting Hen looks on in disbelief. She has hatched out a batch of White Pekin Ducklings? The rooster was no duck, she knew that. What happened? She is perplexed and trying to figure it out. Those eight ducklings are a squeezable hat full that will soon swim away from their mother hen. She will be left standing on shore.*

## Chapter Three
# The Process

Memory reminds me that as a country lad in the early spring time we were always involved with baby chickens and sometimes ducklings. They were our toys, our pets. There were no lifeless, brightly colored plastic make-believe toys, as there are now. The kind that youth play with one day then toss in the toy box where they await the trash collector. Not so with our prized playthings that we took the utmost pride in. These were the first objects shown to visitors in our home. We were proud of the toys we raised—they were alive.

As pre-schoolers we learned to feed, water, and keep their box clean. Oh! They were so cuddly. If anything happened to our living toys we would be brokenhearted and sob all about the place.

As we grew we would have chickens of our own to sell come fall. This would be our Christmas money. It came about so effortlessly with the aid of nature. One would not send away to a hatchery. There was no such commercial business then. We began from scratch either in late winter or early spring. The laying hens would be watched closely. Those that were friendly to a rooster would be called romantic. Consequently, their eggs would be fertile. There was nothing halfway. Hen's eggs are fertile or not fertile. We would mark select hens, save their eggs in trap

*Out of confinement after twenty-one days. What a great big world. My! My!*

nests, take them to the house and keep them in a cool place separate from all others. Just the same as we kept the best ears of open pollinated seed corn for planting come next spring.

These hens were always broody first. When they showed definite intentions of wanting to set, we brought back the eggs from the house and put them in a high clean nest where they were less likely to be disturbed. These were immediately put on a twenty-four hour schedule for twenty-one days. How we looked forward to that day when, by holding one of her eggs to our ear, we could hear a pecking or scratching noise inside. Soon the shell would be pipped and a tiny beak would appear through the opening of a tough egg shell. We would jump up and down with joy in the screened off end of the henhouse. Some chicks in each batch would need a bit of help. We gave each chick a drink of water. Other nourishment, to last a couple of days, was provided by nature from within the egg.

This annual event happened in a nice chicken house, in a shed or other outbuildings, maybe not even on a farm. It happened in odd locations where a hen was also apt to hide her nest. Most families in towns and villages kept poultry as well. Hatching time was always close to Easter. Grass on our back lawn would be greening. Out of confinement would come mother hen and her brood. We would place them in a triangular wood hutch with slats on the front through which the chicks could pass to and fro. We kept the hen in confinement. She had to be watered, fed, and the hutch moved to clean grass each day. This was always my chore, and I did it with pleasure. How they would grow! Like the plants and bugs they were feeding on.

Predators were always a problem. It was not unusual to lose several chicks. Rats, weasels, skunks, raccoons and chicken hawks were always searching out their next meal. Defenseless new chicks were easy prey. Anytime. Barn cats had to be watched, too. The only answer was to lift up the hutch and let the mother hen and her brood go free. She would train her little ones by

*A Plymouth Barred Rock Hen and part of her brood in the straw. All setting hens are great mothers and proud as a peacock, too.*

*A nice clean coop in the country. This is the way chickens are supposed to be kept—not in abandoned small town shacks.*

*These are New Hampshire Reds. They are great meat producers, grow fast and make fryers and broilers. An American Breed.*

sounding her own siren. If she let out a certain warning sound that resembled a high pitched and fast cluck, all her babies would come to her post haste. She would cover them and break the neck of most any varmint that dared to come close. Mother hens are second only to a Canada Goose in this protective trait.

In this manner every farm family in the country, villages, small towns, and even some cities had and raised their own chickens, ducks, or other poultry as desired.

It was because of the convenience. No cook ran to a nearby store when planning the next meal. That source did not exist. In its stead most every family had their own chicken house providing fresh eggs. These eggs could be prepared in many different ways suitable for the main dish for any one of the three daily meals. Everybody liked them and eggs were excellent nourishment for all ages.

Suppose company was coming or a bountiful Sunday dinner just for the immediate family was on the schedule. Fresh meat was needed but refrigeration was yet years into the future. Out to that small pen of young cockerels, being fed for exactly such an occasion, went the cook. She selected an eight pounder. Problem solved. Enough would be left over to pick on for a couple of days.

*A pair of Orgingtons placed here for contrast. This is the sedimentary type that shows up in all species of flesh and blood.*

## Favorite Specimens

*A pair of Plymouth White Rocks. These excellent meat chickens yield a fine roasting carcass free of pinfeathers. White ones do not show at the dinner table. They include all the excellent qualities of the original Plymouth Barred Rocks but do not lay as many eggs. For egg production, one must go to Hybrid White Leghorns, but the world would starve for lack of chicken meat if its production depended on Leghorns.*

In some respects poultry can be the finest and most enjoyable of pets you ever owned. Other situations can easily develop out of this bliss. Instantly, changes can dominate a heavenly mental state.

For example, I raised a certain baby chick until he was losing his fuzz and pinfeathers were beginning to show. His name was Peeper. I named him Peeper because when he was a few days old, if I was any place in his vicinity, he would yell his head off by letting out a string of loud peeps. He followed wherever I went, if he could. One hot, muggy day he followed me into the barn and even up into a horse stall where I intended to harness a team and go in the field. My team was stomping flies. I was a bit fearful for Peeper so I picked him up and tossed him out the barn through an open window. I never gave him another thought. I backed the horses out of their stalls to hook them double out in front of the barn. For some reason I looked down at the cement floor. There was my Peeper flatter than a bride's pancake. He had reentered the stable. His death was instant and painless but it hit me hard between the eyes. I just had the whole of his warm strong body in the palm of my hand when I tossed him out the window to protect him from harm. I am not a fatalist but it was Peeper's day, that entire day. I was his mother and failed my responsibility.

East on Maple Avenue from us lived two girls who also liked to raise a few chickens. Every spring they would start out with a broody Red Rhode Island hen and a dozen or so fertile eggs. This particular year they lost all of their baby chicks to a June freshet storm, except one who survived but had a broken leg. They put a splint on his leg, babied him along and of course he became a pet, grew like a weed, and matured into a beautiful cockerel with a limp.

One morning he was not about their steading and underfoot, as usual. The girls thought nothing of it. That same evening at the Odd Fellow Hall in town there was a box social. Their mother

*This photo of the two participants whose boxes were sold to the young village blacksmith was taken three years before the Box Social. Here is some of their much loved flock. They requested that I not use their names, but you might know who they are. They became wonderful women, as was their mother.*

prepared and decorated a box for each girl. After some home talent entertainment an auction was held with Fred Holland as auctioneer. Glen (Dick) Blanchard, the town's blacksmith, bought both boxes. He sat between the sisters and ate from both their boxes. The food was excellent and a jolly good time was being had by all until one of these sisters took a chicken drumstick from a box. The bone was crooked. She tarried for a moment before taking another bite. She rose, broke down crying, and fled from the hall, followed by almost everyone there. At this point the story had to be told. Most of the crowd left shortly thereafter with tears in their eyes. Their pet had been sacrificed, especially for this box social. The sisters reminded me of this event, and both are now over ninety years old. How's that for folklore?

## Chapter Four
# Potpourri of Ducks and Geese

In their wild state, Mallard Ducklings soon after hatching will tail their mother closely wherever she goes, all in the water, of course. It is amazing that they keep up with her, but they do. She leads them from one reed bed to another where bugs are plentiful. During these meandering hunting forays it is necessary for the brood to be led over some deeper water where danger lurks. The last duckling in line is the most vulnerable. There will be a great splash in the water where he was. It calms. Count your ducklings. There will be only twelve left where there were thirteen. Drakes vanish and never help the hens raise their brood. There are delinquent fathers in Nature, too.

That is why there is a law in our fishing codes prohibiting the use of baby waterfowl as bait. Those large Northerns especially love the tidbits the ducklings provide.

Ducklings are about three weeks old before they spread out in search of food. From then on the hen has trouble keeping the growing brood together until they feather out and fly away. Who is the leader now? The largest and most aggressive young drake. Who brings up the rear? Mother hen duck, an interesting switch-about.

For many years, after establishing a hideaway, we purchased a couple dozen Mallard ducklings and a half dozen goslings from a hatchery. They were nursed along at the main steading downstate until they were large enough to go on their own on the St. Mary's River. Many pleasant and enjoyable incidents happened with these purchased ducklings and some tragedies, also.

One hot muggy day we were bringing a large box of ducklings with us, plus our standard luggage, on a 286 mile trip to our studio and lumber office. The conveyance was full. The livestock in the back was raising a rumpus so we stopped. One duckling had gotten out of the box. The others were clamoring to go, too. They were out of water. Dry ducks are not contented ducks.

The free duckling hopped out of the hatchback as soon as it was opened. While we were trying to catch the one who was hiding in the high grass on the berm of the road, a whole mess of others jumped to the ground. Ducklings were everywhere, some even went on the road. Other drivers noticed our plight and stopped to help. We had a duck roundup in progress. Along came a County Sheriff Deputy on road patrol to direct traffic. Soon everything was under control except a question arose from the officer.

"Where did you get these little wild Mallard ducks? They act wild and look wild."

"These aren't wild Mallards, sir, they came from a hatchery," was my reply.

*Introducing little ones to the big water. Mallard Ducklings afraid of water? Yes. The problem is that they have no Mother Hen Duck to lead, and your author is a poor substitute.*

"I'm giving you a ticket subject to you sending a copy of an invoice of your purchase of these, from a hatchery, to my headquarters within seven days." We could and did, and nothing further was heard. This officer should get a merit badge.

Geese were not of the temperament to go on their own. They used to hang around with us. Before the Native Americans who could prove they were at least 1/32 Indian stripped out our fishing grounds with gill nets, we would go fishing every morning when the weather was agreeable. We had brought up a few domestic geese called White Embden goslings. They would attempt to follow us when we were going out fishing with the boat, but we would soon lose them in the spray. On return it was a different story. They knew the sound of our motor or could identify our boat by sight. When we were a half mile from the dock, they'd make a beeline for us. I never was able to figure that out. We had to take care that one or more of them didn't get

*As it was in the beginning: the great outdoors, a feed dish, water pan, and place of safety. We were no mother to them, so our efforts on their behalf could have been very crude from their point of view.*

cut up in our propeller. Late in the fall one year we had a feather party up the shore a bit at a neighbor's place. We drove four white geese into his garage, dispatched and dry picked their carcasses. All the neighbors who helped got enough down for a new pair of pillows plus a dressed goose as a coupon. It was like old times when country people pooled their resources on most any job that had to be done. It was hard work but great fun, too. Most of those events closed with a square dance that continued into the night or until the applejack was consumed.

At home, after a thunderstorm, a pen of ducklings was missing. The storm had blown down the boards on one side of their pen. The ducklings had vanished into thin air. We looked in all the barns, feedlots, and outbuildings, but found nothing. We checked the roadside for tracks in the mud. Nothing. It had been a wild June freshet and my wife Naoma came up with an idea.

"They will love this warm rainwater. How about the road ditches?"

Several ditches and large tiles converge on the Broadblade Farms building area. They would have to swim against a strong current in whichever direction they took so we hit the free-flowing floodwater ditches. Soon our daughters let out a whoop we all could hear from a distance.

"The lost is found." They ran ahead of the dozen and a half urchins and turned them around. Those little runts were no larger than the palm of your hand. They had swum at least a half mile from the pen at a pace that was faster than a person could walk.

*Two Whiteys, a Pekin duckling and a young Embden goose get into the flowers.*

*This was a different group of pets that possessed some sort of sensors. They would swim out to meet us on the St. Mary's River. How could they know it was us when we were a half mile from shore?*

*Goslings growing like weeds on grain. At this age bugs are not yet their primary food item.*

We always liked to raise a couple of White Pekins with each year's batch of young Mallards. They all traveled the west side of the St. Mary's River between Munuscong Bay south, almost, to Gogomain Bay. The White Pekins were easy to see, so we always knew where the whole clan was. Sometimes the ducklings would make themselves scarce for several days. We would rev up the fishing boat and go searching the shoreline. The White Pekins were always a dead giveaway. We would swing that Alumacraft about and head for our home dock, knowing that when the ducks hankered for grain they would be back to Perk's Pad kitchen door. It was fun raising them. Every day there was something different, just like raising our own kids.

Predators are a twenty-four hour problem with all poultry until they are developed enough, in the direction nature had intended, to provide for their own protection. Various assets are utilized. Some varieties inherit more than one asset to ensure longevity. These include speed in swimming, diving and flying plus camouflage to blend in with the environment in which they live.

However, when young these traits are not sufficiently developed to protect them.

Skunks, weasels and chicken hawks take their toll. Mink are death to ducklings. Larger animals such as fox, coyote and unleashed dogs have all caused us trouble or monetary loss when the ducklings were out of the water.

We had another sad experience at our studio in Chippewa County, Michigan. This was with eleven almost feathered Mallard ducks. This bunch would come home each night. We had a large woven steel mesh cage setting up against the wall of the

Pad near the kitchen door. For their convenience, there was also an outdoor faucet nearby that we would leave dripping. They loved a continuous damp environment. They would congregate around this cage about sunset each day. Before retiring I would make sure they were all inside, close the door and roll a large block of wood against it. This block of wood was too heavy for me to lift.

One morning the sun broke by taking a peak at the St. Mary's River over the high point of St. Joseph's Island. Many photographic professionals capture this shot on a clear morning as a saleable product of their trade. As I stood looking out my bedroom window, I wondered what in the world had moved that large block of wood from our duck pen. The door was swinging wide open. Oh, my ducklings! I was wide awake now, so out I went, barefooted and with my pants half on, to look into their

*We change but little in life. Here is the author at eighty-eight with a recent group of pets—two dozen Mallard Ducks and two Embden Geese. This all goes back to the day I took pet chicken Dode to the Show and Tell at our Ryno Country School when I was six. They still love me.*

*Baby Mallard Ducklings, not far from the shell, already becoming pets or living toys to a pair of teenagers.*

pen—no ducks. There was a black dog in our yard that belonged to a close neighbor. He was chewing on parts of a young duck. He dropped his food and took down the driveway toward his home when I yelled at him. We eventually found what was remaining of our beautiful pen of ducks nearby. We were shocked and discouraged. They were nearly full-feathered.

We carefully examined the block that barred the door. The medium-sized black dog was guilty by association, but even though some bark had been stripped from the block of wood, there had to be something else involved, like a large German Shepherd that often ran about the community unattended with the black dog, or a black bear or wolf. Regardless, we decided to call a halt to the project—we'd had enough grief.

Yet it is pleasing to have a Mallard mother hen bring her brood back to the old feeding grounds. She could be one of those former ducklings I held in the palm of my hand. That bit of gratification makes it all worthwhile. Mark the entire project over a dozen or more years "paid in full."

One year we raised and fed out two hundred White Pekin ducks for the Holiday in our meat market. Behind the cattle feedlot, about eighty rods, was an undrained sag hole where we raised ducks. One late fall morning I was going over that hill with a jag of corn for their self-feeders. Not one duck was moving and they were scattered everywhere. All were dead. I reversed my field and returned to the barn. Nobody believed me. Their bodies were cold; the killing had taken place about midnight. This was a substantial loss. No single predator could have killed them all, some would have escaped.

It could have been a pack of fox, coyotes, or wild dogs. No traces. No clues. The soil was hard enough that the killers left no tracks. We dug a large hole, picked all of them up and tossed them into a common grave. Leprechauns? Demons? Black Angels? What happened?

An ageless fowl poem has been used in various forms of advertising, but the author of the original is unknown. It goes something like this with variations:

> M. R. Ducks
> M. R. Not Ducks
> O. S. A. R.
> C. M. Wings
> L. I. B.
> M. R. Ducks

After a diligent search of possible sources, no information was found as to the author or copyright owner of this poem. It has become a valuable statement of country humor and folklore. It has been about for a few generations. Sincere thanks to the unknown author on behalf of all of us.

*A chicken plant nestled in the orchard. For us it never included laying hens, only meat poultry. It took years to get it together.*

## Chapter Five
# Chicken Roundup

This episode goes back to when I was but a youngster. It was embodied annually with a group of tricks to be executed only on Halloween. There was no such thing as trick or treat for our small group; that was only for girls, sissy boys, and pre-school babies.

There were eight of us boys who would have a list of offenses to settle with businesses, schools, and a few individuals. Our tricks were methodically planned, not property damaging or financially costly. By 11:00 P.M. Halloween night, the job was complete and we all went home because the next day was a school day and we did not want to look as if we had been out all night.

I remember one particular Halloween very well because of what happened as an aftermath about seven decades later. On that Halloween our gang moved considerable traded farm machinery from an implement dealer about town. We didn't forget the schoolhouse, depot waiting room, grain elevator and hay sheds. We had our eye on some corn shocks that somehow walked up on Main Street to form a row from a mail carrier's garden. The town bootlegger's car lost the air in all four tires. The town grouch had "Be Happy" printed with soap on his car windshield. The sugar beet weigh station stove chimney was packed full of sugar beets. Debris from village gardens was stored on the respective owner's porches. The deviltry was ample, but normal for a small country town without a special cop to tail the young life about on Halloween night.

One business family in this village comprised of a young couple. They were so occupied with securing and raising a young family that their general store was sloppy and ill kept in comparison to the competition. Customers overlooked this discrepancy once they met the new owners. They stole most all the business with their pleasing personalities. They bought out what remained of the Dan Reardon estate across from their store. This gave them room to expand, and that they did. Within a couple of years they would take in trade most anything in produce that a farmer had to offer: cream, eggs, poultry, fence rails, baled hay, straw, oats, corn, and garden produce. Their business was not on our depredation list.

My mother and father were among their closest friends. We lived only two doors up the street over Cozadd's Hardware and Lumber Company. The young storekeepers used the Reardon buildings to shelter their excess trading goods. One building was formerly an old community ice house where ice harvested off nearby lakes and streams was packed in new sawdust and sold to customers in the summer to preserve food. There was absolutely no refrigeration except the use of stored ice before electricity came to small towns.

At about the time this young couple went into business, the ice house was not needed. He used it as a live chicken storage. Sometimes he would have as many as two hundred chickens on hand. He fed them well on the grain farmers brought to him in trade. The only bedding these chickens ever had was the cobs from ears of corn, which is practically nothing. He never made an attempt to clean them out, so on some muggy days in summer that ice house, nee chicken coop, smelled so strongly that neighbors who lived close by or downwind could barely stand the odor. It didn't seem to bother the chickens. The ammonia fumes generated by that chicken manure would smart your eyes and burn your skin when a person was hot and sweaty.

Customers would complain to the owner but he took no heed.

Being from the city and untidy by nature, he told those who complained that the weather would change, thus solving this minor problem. Many did not like his answer. Others suggested that he get a couple of his farmer friends and take the chicken manure back to their farms where it would do some good. Others claimed he had no right to keep chickens in confinement in town. People were getting hot on the subject until September came along with cooler weather. Most stopped complaining. However, another summer was languishing in its time. Then the Village would go rotten once more because a storekeeper did not clean out that old ice house half full of chicken manure.

On Halloween night this particular year, I was at home in my bed mulling over the fair job our small group of early teenage boys had done to the town hours before. We considered this our privilege once a year. It was satisfactory, but not enough to impress the public. We had slipped from our parents' control for a few hours. Next thing I knew, my dad was poking me in the ribs and it was daylight.

"Get up, Stan. Get up, hurry."

"What's the matter? Is the hardware on fire beneath us?" He got right to the point.

"Our neighbor called and said John White just phoned that one of the storekeeper's big roosters was on his back porch as the day broke, crowing. Lottie Benjamin, White's housekeeper, did not like that. The storekeeper doesn't like it either because he looked over to the old ice house and the door is wide open."

"Anything else?" I asked.

"Yes, he says your Halloween gang let his chickens out. He wants you to get the boys all over to his store in ten minutes to round up his chickens."

I tried to phone them all but the only ones that showed were the Benear twins, Robert and Raymond. Their mother was strict. She roused them out of bed. They supported me by stating none of us were any place near his stinking old ice house/chicken coop.

Nevertheless, five of us that included the storekeeper, my

dad, and three boys got busy. The owner did not know how many he had, but thought the count would be about a hundred. Soon, between us, we had caught eight, threw them back in the ice house and secured the door. We cornered one on blacksmith Charlie Dunkle's back porch. It was a white Leghorn hen. She escaped us by flying straight up about twenty feet and going for a woodlot nearby. The town's pet dogs had caught at least three and were all enjoying breakfast over fresh chicken.

Town dwellers came out and thanked us boys for letting out the storekeeper's stinking chickens. They had stood the stench all last summer. People thanked and thanked us in appreciation for opening that door, which we DID NOT DO.

We were catching it from both sides, positive and negative, credit and debit. None of our gang, so-called, even touched that door. We were extremely truthful to each other no matter what the penalty might be.

At that same time I was a small businessman as their newsboy. I was all about the homes in Lennon in the course of one day. I knew things about the residences that were going on legal and illegal and kept my mouth shut. Several of the townspeople

*Some chickens were not recovered in the roundup. This pair was lucky to sneak out of the village and back to a friendly farm environment where Rhode Islands were welcome.*

*A couple of old hens, a Barred Rock and a Rhode Island Red, asking each other who opened that icehouse door. They both made their way to safety far out into the beautiful countryside. Now, where do we find a rooster?*

had traces of what happened to that flock of ice house inhabitants. The odor of burning feathers was all over town. Others disposed of inedible parts of chickens by digging a hole in their garden. Freshly turned soil in the Fall is very noticeable, as is blood on a block of wood at the winter woodpile.

The father of one of our gang hit a large, fat rooster on his back porch with a broom handle "right behind the ear." He laid there and quivered until he was secured with a butcher knife from the kitchen cupboard. My brother in crime told me that it made the best chicken dinner they every had. And so it went. Less than a dozen were ever placed back in that filthy building. Eventually it burned. By who and why? It's never been answered.

Some sixty years later we attended the storekeeper's wife's funeral at a church in New Lothrop, another village nearby. Her husband was there with his family of grand and great children. I introduced myself and shook hands with him. He thought a moment, then blurted out loud enough so most people in the church could hear, "Yes, Stan Perkins—you're the one who opened the door on my chickens on Halloween night and cost me a lot of money."

There was nothing I could say, I just walked away. He had harbored that untruth all of more than four generations.

The facts were that more big chicken dinners were served per capita in that village for a week than any other location on this planet—by the best cooks in the world. I wish to wind down this TALE with a couple more facts.

None of our small gang of Halloweeners ever unlatched that door. Also, anyone or a group of people who lived within smelling distance of that rotten building and its contents used Halloween as an opportunity to rid themselves of this putrid scourge. Some adult opened that door and gave our small group of teens all the credit. At this point in my life I wish to thank all those residents of this village still living for thinking so well of our Halloween group during all those years since 1927.

## Chapter Six
# Sticky Stuff

There was a hired hand, Ed Shumory, who worked for my grandfather when the total farm power was horses. His wages, which included room and board, were forty dollars a month. He was trustworthy and neat about the house and his room. However, he had one omission in his hygiene: Ed never cleaned his teeth. He didn't even own a toothbrush. Decaying food would build up on his gums and his breath was often unbearable. Grandkids, like myself, did not hang around him too much.

I always had a few marked pet chickens about the place. They would follow anyone about the yard that paid them much heed. One warm spring Sunday afternoon, after a hard week's work following teams in the fields, Ed laid down on the back lawn and fell sound asleep. We kids were nearby just running about playing tree tag. Ed was snoring really loudly with his mouth open. Must have been Ed's snoring that attracted a pet chicken I called Elmer. Elmer came over and started to peck at Ed's teeth. He liked what he got and went back several times for more as we watched from out of sight and sound. Elmer was lucky he escaped with his life as Ed nearly clamped down on the chicken's head. Mum was the word, and we never said anything. I don't believe Ed ever knew we were watching.

Geese are often used to weed gardens and crops. They are selective with their grazing habits and this trait makes them as attractive as their eggs, meat, and especially livers. One feature, or dessert, of a chicken's diet is lice found on hogs, especially on the back and insides of their ears. Chickens and hogs are tolerant of each other. Smart farmers, before the advent of the chemical age, were alert to this association between chickens and hogs. Hogs are sloppy in their eating habits and hurry to get their share at the trough or self-feeder. Nature controls that problem, and chickens utilize food wasted by hogs at both ends. Hogs can follow cattle and take care of waste ration both undigested and digested, which means poultry is the final cleanup battalion.

Horn flies are a nuisance and a costly irritant to cattle in certain seasons of the year. When cattle lay down to rest and/or chew their cud, chickens will pick off those pesky horn flies. This remains a non-chemical solution to a profit stealing problem. This home remedy, which aids cattle feeding and milk production, is performed by chickens. Again, a support from Nature.

Chickens are not all positive. At times they can die like flies from simple changes in the weather or a windblown virus that the owner has little or no control over. Sometimes chickens can be downright troublemakers. Even enough to break up a good, solid marriage. There was a devoted farm couple who shared life together until a beautiful pet Rhode Island Red rooster, that was hatched, raised, and had the run of the steading, changed things. There was only one place he would roost. It was on a certain barrel in the woodshed attached to the back of the house near the kitchen. When he was small, it made little difference where he spent the nights, but as he grew and matured, he also developed a mind and body of his own. The couple did not like him to roost in the woodshed because he made a large mess every night, which the wife had to clean every morning. It was her job. A nasty job. This bird should have been roosting in the barn where the farmer would have to clean up the mess. There it mattered little whether he cleaned it up or not. They decided, in order to keep peace in the family, to shut Red out of the woodshed. They had no sooner assumed restful positions in bed when they heard a terrible noise at their bedroom window. It startled them.

"Mother, what was that?"

"You'd better look out," she retorted gingerly, "maybe someone is in trouble and needs help." He looked out, but saw nothing.

In the meantime she had used the chamber pot and did not slide it way back under

### The Culprit

*This Rhode Island Red Rooster was young, strong, and set in his place to go to roost before dark each evening. He eventually broke up a solid marriage.*

the bed. He tipped it over and the contents spilled out onto an ancient ingrained carpet. It was over wide pine flooring and would take months before the odor would leave. He made a bunk out in the woodshed and decided he would spend the night there. He was getting settled down again when that red rooster started a rumpus outside the woodshed door. He gave up and let in the bird. Red immediately assumed his usual roosting place on the rim of the barrel that contained flour for baking. The farmer quickly dozed off to sleep.

When wife Angela came out in the morning to get flour for a batch of pancakes, she let out a shriek and an oath that woke up and downgraded sleepy farmer Fred. He had let Big Red into the woodshed and then fell asleep. She was always careful and turned the rooster just so, so he pooped in a five gallon bucket, but Fred was not as conscientious. Red had done a lot of pooping inside the flour barrel and ruined most of it. Angela wanted the dirty old red rooster killed right then and there. He would make a large batch of tough chicken soup. Farmer Fred refused. One thing led to another and they eventually divorced. The case was closed by the judge saying, "Divorce granted, because of irreconcilable difference over the toilet habits of a pet Rhode Island Red Rooster."

There was a neighbor boy who grew up on an adjoining farm. He liked chickens and could hardly wait each spring until the first new chicks began struggling to get out of their shells. His mother could never go out to the henhouse to gather eggs without Kenny going along. He loved to gather eggs.

Once when Kenny was helping with the eggs he began looking all about the henhouse floor. He searched out every niche. Finally his mother, Jenny, asked, "Kenneth, what are you looking for?"

Without looking up he replied, "My gum."

"Your gum?"

"Yes, my gum! I only can have one stick a week, as you know. This stick was only half chewed and it popped out of my mouth in here yesterday."

"Kenneth, you stop looking right here and now. There is nothing on this floor to put in your mouth or even touch with your hands."

"Yes, I know, Mother."

"How do you know, son?"

"Gum tastes much better."

One family moved to our community from Ohio and introduced an Easter custom that I cannot overlook: Eggs. Youngsters in the family would hide a cache of "hen fruit" before Easter. On Easter morning eggs were brought out of hiding and revealed to the adults. A private holiday festival would then take place. Eggs were first boiled, cooled and colored as table decorations. Many were consumed. Eggs were prepared in many ways, even marinated. Before they were all eaten everybody swore off eggs for a long time—we were so sick of eggs!

Nearby was a family of chicken farmers who had been pinned down for weeks one year. They desperately needed several days away from their confining business. Only a few tasks were imperative: feeding a thousand laying hens, gathering the eggs, preparing them for market and checking the proper adjustment in the ventilating system. This had to be manually controlled to keep the flock comfortable regardless of the outside weather conditions.

A young man who was a senior in high school and had occasionally worked for them before was left in charge. Being an executive now, he secured a couple of friends to do the actual labor. Gathering eggs, washing them as needed and placing them in the thirty-dozen sized cases soon became monotonous. The temptation was too great for their undeveloped mentalities to resist. They began tossing eggs to each other. A few were thrown a little harder, some were broken. Gradually it turned into an egg fight. That was something these subnormal town kids had always wanted to do: have a friendly egg fight at someone else's expense.

A neighbor lady, whom the owners had asked to check out the egg plant at her convenience, just happened to arrive. She intercepted a couple of missiles before getting the rascals' attention, but not before they had destroyed a full case of thirty dozen eggs.

The owners had to be called back from their vacation. The culprits vanished into thin air. The young man in charge had left for a bit to see his girlfriend. The cleanup was costly, not only because of the eggs lost, but the drudgery labor-wise. Everything had to be cleaned from floor to ceiling and dried egg yolk is like glue—when dry it becomes almost permanent.

The owners lost heart. They were still in business but egg production lost its upbeat and was never able to regain its former status with them. It closed, in my opinion, directly because of this costly incident. It was an expensive type of entertainment by a couple of irresponsible young yokels. Although they were responsible, those destructive young men were never punished.

The next account is about "Ego," a racehorse who did not make the big time. Ego's speed as a racehorse never materialized, but his mentality was exceptional. His grandsire was the great Man Of War and a full brother to the successful Trigger. Ego's dam was owned by the Ford family. He was sold cheap because he was a buckskin, not the palomino they desired. A resident of Milford, Michigan bought Ego and he became a pet. This horse was very intelligent and followed his new owner about like a dog. Once, when the owner was replacing glass in his chicken coop windows, Ego licked all the fresh putty from the new windows without removing glazer points or breaking the glass. He became very cunning and later mischievous, as a native Wolverine. He was known to take hand tools from the tool box, in his mouth, and scatter them about the yard. Once he came upon a heavy wrecking bar and tossed it on the back porch.

Above all, he did not like chickens. Ego would reach over the chicken lot fence and catch one in the corner, if possible, then let it loose on the outside. The owner wondered how his chickens kept getting out. He examined the fence closely and found no holes. Soon after the owner was making a fast trip to the outside privy when a hen came at him from over the chicken coop. He caught Ego, and the problem was solved. The horse had grabbed a hen in his mouth and tossed her high enough that she flew over the roof out of fright.

Ringling Brothers, Barnum and Bailey tried to buy the rascal, but the owner wouldn't sell. Ego was a pet.

---

Long ago, when my family existed as sustenance farmers, there was always an old truck about the premises. Annually we would rev up this conveyance and round up all the scrap iron on the farm and often some from our neighbors. We took this to a junkyard in the city and sold it. After a few years we became well-acquainted with the owner of the yard, a Jewish gentleman, and I mean gentleman. In conversation he became aware that we kept a few hundred chickens. One thing led to another and we invited him to come out to our place. He drove out in his Cadillac that was so long he could hardly fit in our small driveway. His car was full of kids, none over ten years old. They got out of the car with him and were a very curious bunch. Coming out to a real farm was a big deal that provided them with questions and much physical activity.

The father had different ideas—he wanted to see our chickens. It was about sundown and the chickens were going to roost. He went down the roost feeling all the heavy old hens.

"Yes, Mr. Perkins. We could use several of these large hens. Would you sell me some?"

"Sure," was my father's reply.

We suggested the market price at that time. He promptly offered us a dollar more, each, but only wanted those with a large gob of fat in their rear ends. To us they were free loaders, not layers. We were pleased to rid ourselves of these free riders. We got a couple of old burlap fertilizer bags and he found eight hens he could use. We put both bags in the trunk of that gorgeous Cadillac. He rounded up the kids, counted noses, and was gone. In two weeks he was back with the same sacks for a refill. We were curious. We asked our fat hen customer what in the world he had done with them.

"Our rabbi koshers them for us. Then we render out the fat and use it as shortening in our cooking," he told us. We read up on the subject a bit and learned that Jewish people extensively use chicken fat in their cooking. Thus we found a good market for our fat old hens, thanks to our friend. This made chickens that were almost discards equally as valuable as the strong young cockerels.

*The Orpington chicken is a large breed whose white skin makes it popular. The Buff Orpington is the best known and was pleasing to our Jewish customers.*

Years ago, because of the large amount of hand labor required to farm a half section of land, extensive amounts of hired help was required, both male and female. They came from the large families of nearby neighbors. The period of employment was usually for the season. Once an extra child, one not needed at home, had completed the eight grades offered by the one room country school, s/he was considered eligible to leave home and seek local employment. The homes were large. Four hired men made it necessary to have two hired girls. All lived under one roof, including the owner's family. It was sailed as a tight ship, except on some rainy days.

Pranks and acts of nature were difficult to control or suppress. The owner's wife was the law inside the big house. Sleeping rooms were upstairs on both sides of a long hall. In the hall was a partition. It had an unusually heavy door with a padlock whose key was kept only in the housewife's apron pocket. That door was opened only during the morning cleanup, and re-locked when the beds were made.

An enterprising young farmhand with assistance from a screwdriver bypassed the imposing padlock. The owner's wife was not aware of this mischief until the door became loose at the hinges because the screw holes became worn. An in-house romance had been carried on with eggs used as their communication method. Boiled eggs were a common main course. If her lover's eggs were served soft boiled that would be a no go. If they were hard boiled he would be welcome the following night. This was better than the Morse Code for privacy!

There was another chicken-related sign used on a local farm. A favorite hired man would normally wear a large straw hat in the field to shield himself from the sun's rays when following a team. It was a necessary item. Once two hired girls swiped it for a few days, and it was later found by the owner well occupied. Hired girls always gathered the eggs. They secured a broody hen setting on a nest of eggs about ready to hatch. This whole caboodle was moved carefully to the barn while the men were in the field. The driving horse's manger was not in use, so it was a perfect setting for the missing straw hat, the pipping eggs, and finally the broody hen. All was made to look as if she had been setting there for the full twenty-one days. The hat's owner knew better; some female was teasing him. It took a few weeks to sort her out, but he did eventually. They were married within a year. Financial help from both their families and a bank mortgage started them on life's highway. It all began with a batch of baby chickens in his straw hat. Sneaky? Yes! However, in a crude, early American pioneer way, she used a willing setting hen as a tool. This hired girl soon became a housewife in her own modest home. The male in this romance was not the instigator, as the picture on the next page would lead one to believe.

*This was lifted from a newspaper cartoon at least sixty years ago, framed and presented to your author at a banquet. Both the Artist and Publisher are unknown.*

# Chapter Seven
# Poultry Poachers and Chicken Thieves

Never have I heard of anyone being arrested and convicted of stealing poultry to alleviate the pangs of hunger. As a justice of the peace for a decade, never was a case of that character brought before me. However, I suppose it has happened.

In yesteryear, swiping a chicken or other fowl off a roost was thought to be in the category of a Halloween prank. It was common for three or four couples to get together in agreeable weather and have a chicken roast. Some of them would go to a secluded, prearranged spot and build a fire, cut two small, green trees, each with a crotch, drive them into the ground and place a green pole that a chicken or other fowl could be impaled upon between them. After cleaning and dressing a chicken carcass or two, they would place it on this spit to cook as they slowly turned the pole over hot coals. The aroma from the browning meat whetted appetites. It was not unusual for some member of the group to just happen to fetch along a mouth organ or a banjo. A merry time was had by all at the unknown expense to some farmer who maintained a goodly flock of poultry.

The girls would fetch along a couple loaves of crusty, homemade bread. Dessert would be a generous hunk of maple sugar. There would be plenty for everyone. The variety of their menu was limited but they had each other; early country courting and poultry snitching went hand-in-hand. Life oftentimes began here.

*Poultry was always easy to get at on a farm where the henhouse was usually open twenty-four hours a day. Here the door is left open for early crowers.*

Another group we considered poultry snitchers was the Gypsies. These nomads were smiths, traders, peddlers, fortune tellers and, so we thought, thieves. According to their principles, their taking was not stealing. As a small pre-school child I remember them well. Mothers would phone ahead to warn of their coming on the party line.

"Gypsies are on the way, get your kids inside the house."

A rumor had started, down the road, that this clan was bad and had been trying to snatch farm kids. Nothing of this nature actually took place—it was just plain gossip.

There would usually be two or three small covered wagons with some of the clan walking behind. They would stop at every place and let their thin horses graze while the men and women went to the houses and barns. They were always polite and very social, but became more bold and belligerent the longer they stayed. They employed different tactics as they moved along. Three or four women would gang up on the farmer's wife and try to tell her fortune, which she already knew: Life for a country wife was rough. One would do that while the remainder, having made their entrance, would ransack the house. A half dozen men and boys would do the same outdoors. A lone farmer would have more than he could handle. Consequently they would make off with some poultry, a small pig or a half-grown lamb. Some were horse traders.

The Gypsy leader would give the high sign. Immediately the clan would start for the wagons with their booty. It was a well-rehearsed operation with the leader of the group coming up with a string of colored glass beads for the farmer's wife to ease any trouble. They would always shove off with at least eggs and a couple fat hens. The largest gamble was to get the Gypsy wagons down the road a few miles before night set in so the owner would not have to stay up all night with his shotgun.

*A lad called young Perk is hand shelling corn for a beautiful flock of Plymouth Barred Rock laying hens. There is a brooder house of early vintage in the background, in front of the cattle, sheep, and horse barns. This is how and where the idea germinated—I grew up liking fowl of all description.*

Most country boys have participated in the prank of "cooning" melons, grapes, and any other excess garden produce they could use. Melons were the most sought after—they are so good when cooled. A nearby cold spring served the purpose. The melons would have to be hidden there for about twenty-four hours before cooled down to an edible temperature.

"Melons for tomorrow night. What's for tonight?"

"A chicken roast, okay? Their big fat daughter can't even

count—they'll never miss a brace of chickens."

And so it was, a couple chickens left their happy home. Pieces were soon being roasted over a hot fire on slender green willow branches.

"What fun, spring cooled watermelons tomorrow night. Can't wait—see you there."

There is a tool that can be made best from a piece of heavy wire about six feet long. Bailing wire is too limber. Fashion a flared hook on one end that will fit a chicken's leg. Other sized hooks can be easily made to fit turkeys, geese, and ducks. It's simply a homemade tool to aid in selecting individuals from the flock without causing stress to all of them or causing a noticeable negative commotion.

A certain person used to carry a set of poultry hooks in his buggy. Poultry would often be strung out along a gravel road picking up certain sized stones for their gizzards. Chickens were accustomed to being around horses. This poultry snitcher would pick up chickens with his hook without leaving the driving lines and place his quarry in a crate he kept under the buggy seat. Automated thievery, almost. Snitched fowl were never sold, just used.

There was a local poultry buyer that made an above average living circulating about three or four counties in central downstate Michigan. It was a fertile area for his small business, as most of his providers never surmised. This all took place before there was a conveyance called a pickup. He was ahead of that crowd. Lennie altered an early Model T Ford touring car that had seen its best days. He ripped out the back seat body section and built up a space that would accommodate four chicken crates with room left for a couple spare tires. The material that was formerly the black canvas top was attached to the back of the front seat to provide protection from the weather. While on the road he often lived in his front seat. He ate there, slept, and spent rainy days there. When people saw him coming or going they felt sorry for him. Lennie, sometimes called L.E., was always clean, showered, and as neat looking as possible considering his lifestyle. Farm women loved him and most likely fed him well. They planned on his biannual stops. He was a precursor of the small businessman.

Farm women and farmers' wives had little contact with the outside world. One of their cherished contacts was the merchandise mail order catalogs. Large publications were sent to most farm homes in the Midwestern United States by Sears and Roebuck and Montgomery Ward, though there may have been others. These would be from two to three inches thick and were never discarded when a new one arrived. The old catalog would be placed in the outside privy because of the fine quality paper they were printed on. Women in the country would finger through these great publications page by page comparing quality and cost. Unfortunately, they had no money to send in with their order.

This is exactly where Lennie the itinerant poultry buyer entered the picture. Every farm had chickens and usually other poultry that these country women had set as eggs. Her husband never knew how much poultry was about the steading. Sooner or later L.E. would show with his catching wire hook. In the meantime, these country women and daughters had figured out exactly how much cash they needed to send in their mail order.

For chickens Lennie would pay ten cents a pound according to his estimated weight. His scales were always broken. Geese and ducks he did not prefer because they required so much care before resale. He had a limit of one dollar for tom turkeys and smaller turkeys, including hens, scaled on downward. Often he would be given ducks and geese to seal a deal. Trouble was, L.E. had no competition. Business became larger. He had to put a trailer behind the Model T.

When he got the fowl home he changed hats and became a seller instead of a buyer. His business was located somewhere between Venice Center and Montrose, but no one seemed to know exactly where. He would dress out poultry at night and take it to meat markets in Flint the next morning. Since there was no refrigeration, it had to be moved into consumer channels immediately. He had the operation down to a science. The bird would be stuck in the neck, hung up to bleed out, scalded and feathers removed. He'd then toss it into a barrel of cold spring water for the night without removing either the head or feet. He lost only blood and feathers that had little weight. For this portion of his business he always had working scales. The poultry would come out of that cold spring water weighing very close to their live weight. A hot scalded body took up that cold water. He was never known to have cheated anyone, but was simply a hardshelled buyer and a knowledgeable seller.

Lennie never enjoyed life as most people are want to do. His enjoyment was in his labor. When he died and his estate was probated, the amount of assets he had accumulated was unbelievable. A provision provided that his estate be returned to institutions of higher learning that were prominent within the area. He has a grandson who has his Ph.D. and labors in the livestock industry.

As a sequel to this unique person's life, the relief from bondage he provided for dozens of oppressed country women must not be overlooked and could be his greatest accomplishment. It took many coins to buy merchandise when a dollar was valuable. For half of that dollar one could mail order a pair of blue denim bib overalls with suspenders that would outlast a year of rough usage. Lennie knew those women did not need a lot of money to order what they wanted in the catalog. Poultry raised on a farm by the woman and her kids was theirs as a rule. There were a few despots who would not accept that, but they were in an extreme minority. Most men would be on a back forty cutting brush or tearing up more land to work when Lennie arrived. They never cared about who their wives sold a few chickens to or for how much. This became the leading edge that eventually led to the liberation of womanhood. The few coins—ten, twelve, or sometimes fifteen cents—was all they needed except at Christ-

*A beautiful coop with metal ventilators converted into an outstanding 4-H swine project headquarters. Champion and Blue Ribbon winners are coming out that door come Fair Time. Poultry houses are adaptable.*

mas time. Before Thanksgiving Lennie would loosen his purse strings a bit to provide for the Holidays. Everyone at the steading, including the hands hired by the month and the women who worked in the big house, received gifts.

L.E. traveled his routes continuously, always looking like a tramp. Some children might fear him unless they had seen him before. His Model T was temperamental and would get hot and stall. He had two daughters, Myrtie and Loleta. Often with the spark retarding lever adjusted a bit lower they would take turns spinning it with a hand crank. They could always start it after L.E. had given up. He often said those kids made him feel helpless.

One morning before he could get on the road, a pair of young men with soft hands appeared at his humble abode. They were carrying between them an old slated chicken crate. It was filled with a dozen red pullets. They wanted to sell them. "Okay, let's see what you have."

The old crate included young pullets with some pinfeathers. His scales were still broken, and he was in a hurry to get going.

"These young birds will not weigh over three pounds apiece and they are full of pinfeathers. Thirty-five cents each is all I would pay for them." The sellers looked at each other, took his offer, and soon disappeared down his lane. They left the old crate.

In his poultry buying travels Lennie picked up all kinds of gossip, some old, some new. Other tales were nothing but old wives' concoctions. One story he heard put him to thinking. A pair of young fellows had been caught red-handed siphoning gasoline from a farmer's barrel and carting it off in five gallon cans. The sheriff hauled them up before the local Justice of the Peace and they spilled the whole story, claiming only fools work to earn money, they had an easier way. Until they were caught, it worked.

Lennie put two and two together. He knew the Justice and went to visit him. He told Judge Post about buying a crate of chickens from a pair of likely looking young fellows who appeared out of nowhere. It would be most unusual to imagine the birds were stolen; nothing like this ever happened in the country. Everything and anything was safe where it was left. Crime was unknown.

The parents of the two young men had begged them off from the gasoline transgression. Gas was only eight to ten cents per gallon with no tax. It was considered a minor infringement that their parents settled for. Until they were questioned about the chicken deal they made with L.E. This broke the case wide open. They had been living off the fat of the land, mostly country folks, for a couple of years without sweating a brow. They confessed where they stole the chickens. Lennie knew the owners they mentioned and rushed to their steading. He gave them five dollars for their pullets. He didn't want to be accused, along with the thieves, for buying stolen property.

He heard no more for a few weeks, but then met Judge Post on the road and asked what happened with the case. "Lennie, the case with those two big city brats is still unsettled. They had a crime wave going with all their petty thievery. They are not hardened criminals but can not be released scot-free. We don't want any more of this going on, but I don't know what to do with them."

"Will you turn them over to me for a couple of weeks?" asked Lennie.

"It all depends. What do you have in mind?"

"I have a ditch on my property that drains a pothole. It should be dug two feet deeper to do the job expected. It is forty rods long. I would pay them a daily wage, if they finish the job, by a check made out jointly to them and your court for expenses it has incurred on their behalf. It will teach them what it is to earn a day's pay for a day's honest labor—or they can go to jail for ninety days. Be sure they understand both options. No way do they go free."

"Well put. I'll let you know soon."

The oddball that he was, L.E. made friends and men out of these two waywards. Afterwards they would help with the chicken business as extra hands for scalding and pulling feathers. It made everyone in Lennie's circle of customers smile. He never commented on these petty thieves. They were amply corrected and turned out to be good citizens.

Our countryside do-gooder began business by selling fresh eggs to a store on Asylum Street in west Flint. It included only dressed poultry later and was a community business for about a third of a century. The Genesee County Health Department forced its closure when the owner refused to build separate male and female bathrooms for a half dozen part-time employees. This was the word, at least, that was passed about by his associates.

L.E. had other accounts that were carried with some of his customers. One in particular could never seem to catch up. L.E. was no banker. He could not carry a customer along forever so he devised a plan of his own. On this wholesale customer's invoice he added five dollars more than what his other customers were paying each week. Usually he added it to the largest item listed. After about six months this delinquent buyer came to Lennie and said, "I'd like to pay up that back bill I owe you."

"Sorry, customer, you owe me no bill."

Lennie let him ponder that for awhile, then brought out some old invoices that had all been marked "Paid In Full." The customer was momentarily furious when he realized what had happened, but it was a creative lesson that there is more than one way to skin a cat.

One early morning before the sun rose, Lennie visited his abattoir and loaded up his orders for a big Friday. Driving carefully with a well-loaded trailer tailing his trusty Model T, he glanced at an unknown scroungey animal in the narrow road ahead. Disregarding the beast, he pulled up close to the kitchen door. There were pancakes, pork sausage, and gravy with maple syrup. He stuffed himself well—this was better than when he began the poultry business. It was crackers and cheese on the run then. He closed the kitchen door quietly after giving his one and only cook a thank you on the cheek.

Before mounting his steed and trailer for the day, he took a quick look about. It was devastation. Dressed chickens were everywhere. Most of the sealed boxes had been broken into. He sat on the trailer tongue and cried like a baby from sheer shock before he could notify anyone.

Saying nothing, he went through the kitchen to the fireplace and grabbed his cap and ball off its bracket, frightening the whole family. Out he went, slamming doors in his path. Into the thicket he plunged. He ran out to the road, but nary a twig moved. Luckily no person or being was there—they would have gone to a heavenly or devilish home. His trigger finger was twitching. Soon his family and neighbors gathered about to help. They had heard the commotion, which was uncommon in Lennie's steading, and knew something was amiss.

Very few dressed chickens were saleable. Some varmint! Some dastardly bastard that his mother would not even own. A few chicken carcasses were nearly consumed, but others had just been tossed out in the dirt. The chickens were wet, having been removed from the overnight cold water treatment within the hour. It was a substantial financial loss, and care had to be taken to ensure it never happened again.

Various causes were suggested: a pack of wild dogs, a couple of black sow bears with their hungry young. Coyotes would not and could not cause such destruction in such a brief time, then completely vanish, but a large pack of wolves could. Lennie liked his own idea of the culprits best: a pair of wolverines. As he cooled down and thought it out, he remembered what crossed his path coming up the knoll to the kitchen. It was low to the ground with much shaggy disarranged dark hair. A few were still about, he had seen them before in the distance. They are devious, very destructive, and hate humans to the bottom of their pads. By the time he had left his breakfast door they could have been a quarter mile gone. Mean and crafty.

The loss was made up the next week, but the Who and Why was never solved. After that incident, L.E. always loaded up the trailer after breakfast. That morning's was a great breakfast, perhaps the most expensive he ever stopped to eat. It had to be a pair of dastardly wolverines. To L.E., it was revolting that they were our State Animal.

*A laying coop with hens in the windows decorated with flowers in bloom. Rhubarb and flowers do well around chickens, but poultry manure must be used sparingly. It will burn most plants.*

## Chapter Eight
# Granny's Luscious Meals

The poultry businesses, beginning with the twentieth century, changed in all of its ramifications. This came on gradually. For hundreds of years it had existed as a family business worldwide. An essential commodity was easily swept up in the business revolution that involved us all. By the century's end a large percentage of the poultry business was wrapped up tightly in a few multimillion dollar corporations. This was no surprise; most small, individually owned businesses suffered the same fate.

We, as a family, liked and raised a few fowl of the various species. The skids were greased for us to go commercial in an unusual manner. In June of 1931 I graduated from Flint Central High School among eleven hundred students. The competition was not too strong. I picked up a scholarship in America History that was a two way proposition. The first was a matching grant to work in the southwestern United States and Mexico unearthing early Indian artifacts. In no way could I use this one because of our financial condition—I was needed at home. The other part of the award was more interesting. It was a twenty-five dollar gold piece in a velvet case from The Daughters of the American Revolution. This was at the bottom of the depression following the Stock Market Crash of 1929 and a Bank Holiday coming on. Gold was cheap, only thirty-five dollars per ounce, but it would buy a heap. Who had money? I did. Now the price of gold is depressed from what it was two years ago and is down to two hundred and ninety dollars per ounce, but in any market I had over one half ounce.

From the beginning there was no question about what I wanted to spend it on. I made a beeline for Fred Stevens Hatchery, east of Swartz Creek, at the corner of Elm and Maple Avenues, where a McDonalds now does a great business. Fred traded me two thousand Plymouth Rock baby chicks for my gold piece and I was in business. We lost quite a few because of inadequate equipment and ignorance but fed the remainder out to broiler size and sold them on the Detroit City Market to wholesale buyers. They made us a handsome profit.

A good business venture deserved more of the same. Before I was twenty we purchased a real chicken plant from a retired gentleman in Bancroft, a nearby town. We used a contractor to move it eleven miles and place it on our foundation. It was two stories, a hundred feet long with a feed room in the middle. The entire cost was one thousand dollars. We used this building for many years for poultry meat production. We never were in the egg business, but in beef cattle on a small scale.

As I matured from a slip of a boy at sixteen years to manhood, each year my interest in poultry diminished. There were too many details and working with too small units. It was obvious that production of meat was my bag, but with a larger, more valuable species. Cattle. I had plunged into the chicken business about the same time Tyson's did. They stuck to it and became one of the greatest food providers of the land.

Out of the clear blue came this industrial revolution that provided all our needs. The serenity of country life was abruptly terminated. Strength and dependability and the background of folklore that was the core of this nation were damaged. Nothing escaped. Few worked for themselves. They labored outside their homes, both men and women. Having common interests and chores begot unity. We lost it here.

Poultry raising is a perfect example of a minority industry. A real down-home, backyard enterprise that could absorb the in-

*A larger poultry business than necessary for immediate family use. This is a semi-commercial operation with a feed room in the small barn with the hipped roof at the end. One time it was a source of an individual farmer's income. Not so now. He works off the soil in a shop.*

terest of all family members. It yielded food and fiber. It has been eliminated. Thousands of family projects, in other fields, have suffered the same fate. Commercialization of small businesses has disrupted the family. Fifty percent of marriages fail. At one time, throughout the countryside, divorce was considered a disgrace. Today divorce and broken families lifts the participants into an elite category of society. Juvenile delinquency and youth crimes of today were unheard of before. It is now a major concern and rightfully so. When basic folklore reigned supreme and small solid businesses occupied all family members, our communities were secure. Small family projects balance the world's morality and economy. To operate successfully we must depend on each other, one's close neighbors and our community. It is called Folklore Endeavor.

Let's return to the chicken as our common denominator. It is a lowly bird with pinfeathers. Chickens are almost universal worldwide. It matters little where their home is located. It could be in the depths of a wilderness, on a well-used trail in the great west, in a village or even a city. They are a staple. They provide eggs that can be used as a main course for breakfast, lunch, or dinner. Mechanical refrigeration has not been available for very long, and for much of world history, ice was the only coolant to preserve food. Consequently, fresh fowl of all descriptions has always been convenient and close right in your own backyard. There were few large flocks of fowl other than wild birds such as quail or prairie chickens.

Grain was the limiting factor. It was difficult to produce, requiring a large amount of hand labor. In many instances it had more value than coin of the realm. After cleaning a speck of soil, grain was planted about stumps and undrained, malaria-infested potholes. Cattle, horses, poultry and people all needed grain to keep the starvation specter from haunting both barn and home. It was a serious balancing act. As a result, fowl had to rustle around the edges of forests where they were constant prey of predators. On the other hand, progress was being made, cities grew. Stricter sanitation had to be instituted to protect the general health. This brings us to one of the most important people ever to serve the public in Michigan, Samuel Pearce Duffield,

*Everyone used to keep a few choice chickens in buildings like this. Now they sit idle or used as catchalls. A small flock about fed themselves by picking up their nourishment on the go.*

founder of Parke Davis Chemical company and Health officer of Detroit.

Duffield outlawed the keeping and raising of domestic poultry within the city limits. He had wood sewer lines put into use and encouraged streetcars. This cured a menacing fly problem that breed in the manure piles behind every horse barn. Other large cities followed his lead in sanitation. His methods were copied and a cleanup followed in most mid-sized towns, eventually trickling on down to villages. Now most all incorporated areas comply, and the keeping of poultry and other livestock within the town limits, as well as in many townships, is prohibited.

However, the world's appetite for poultry remained undiminished. It had become the important item in the universal diet as customers waited in food lines. Enterprising entrepreneurs sensed a need, and out of this demand large corporations were formed. Raw materials for this market were scarce. Integrated plants were placed in operation. Consequently, a great business has become well entrenched.

Turkeys are the leader in the current low cholesterol food race. They have taken over the processed food division in food markets. They are many times larger than the largest chickens and easy to bone out. They're not as greasy as either a duck or a goose. Many trade name consumer items today are made from tom turkeys. Chickens are also presented to the general public in several forms: breasts, thighs, drumsticks, wings, etc.

Poultry, collectively, is giving the red meats a run for the future. The latest figures on tonnage consumed are running neck and neck. This has taken place only recently. Neither shows evidence of giving ground. There never will come a time when winner takes all. The world appetite loves them both. There will always be a good market for both red meat and meat from birds that hold their flying down to a minimum, including chickens, turkeys, geese, and ducks.

Chicken is the most understandable and common example of this type of nourishment, but the new type of poultry farming has drastically changed the taste of this meat. Tears could be

*A couple of wild turkey gobblers. They are making a wonderful comeback from near extinction. This great game bird provides a different flavor than secured from the Tom Turkeys fed on chemicals and purchased at a grocery store.*

shed for the person who is not old enough or does not remember the flavor and food quality of yesteryear. How delicious it used to taste. The resulting satisfaction provided was second to none. It has been said that eating is the only activity man can participate in without fatigue. The flavor is an extra coupon. During my lifetime there has been a revolutionary switch in business procedure, and when the family operations changed to monstrous corporations, the flavor of the chicken that's on your table suffered.

Integrated poultry projects were very popular for a few years and provided a stepping stone. They filled the gap in production between the individual family flock and the monster commercial operations that have taken over ninety percent of this particular business today.

With the integrated system, pullets, ready to lay, were put in the batteries at $1.73 per bird. They would lay one hundred percent with full speed ahead for fourteen weeks, eating a super laying mash purchased from the lessor. At the end of fourteen weeks, a flatbed truck piled high with empty chicken crates would pull up. Experienced men would strip the metal batteries of all the hens, place them in crates on the truck, and then head on

*Interior views of an integrated egg plant with the batteries loaded with hybrid layers already producing. This plant was for 1500 birds.*

down the road to the scales. These chickens would be used to make chicken soup with rice or noodles. The operator of this small integrated, egg laying poultry plant would be given credit for this salvage at six cents per pound. This was about twenty-five cents each. He was also expected to have the premises cleaned and disinfected within seventy-two hours. At this time another truck was supposed to appear with a load of new layers with which to restock the plant and immediately place it back into full egg production. Round and round it went and where it stopped only the creditors knew.

Because of their forced environment in crowded steel cages, contrary to all the laws of nature, and a no-choice chemical laying mash, the product is below standard. Visual identification tells you it is a chicken egg. A blindfolded portion placed in your mouth might yield a wild guess. The flavor is completely

*External view of a typical integrated family-sized poultry enterprise that operated under contract for egg production.*

lost in a maze of chemicals used to doctor up the hen's mash. These worn-out hens, when slaughtered, must be combined with other foods, strong seasoning, and too much salt to make a marketable product. Lately, chicken breasts are being sold separately at a premium price.

In my opinion the entire undertaking is grotesque. Call me agriculture's Ralph Nader if you wish; I would be flattered. Eggs have quality plus an individual flavor. The public is not being fooled. Several generations have consumed eggs with nothing for comparison. They don't actually and honestly know the different or that any even exists. Why do discriminating consumers scour the countryside searching out quality? A few do know. Hang in there. Help is on the way with "Fowl Tales"—this travesty has gone on long enough.

Hordes of our populace race from one eatery to another seek-

*An exhausted layer trying to remain atop a pile of eggs she produced in one season. The operator is in the background egging her on.*

*Here are mass-produced baby chicks from an incubator. Using nature's method to hatch with setting hens is obsolete. It is still done as a hobby or in experimental situations only. Otherwise this is a mass-production food industry top to bottom.*

ing dishes prepared by famous chefs with international reputations. These connoisseurs never seem to find what they seek for the simple reason that they do not know what is missing. We do! The best antidote they can reach for is to down two or three martinis before eating, which improves the palatability of food for any diner. In spite of the ability of great chefs, famous restaurants and thousands of down-home wives and mothers, it isn't possible to approach the perfection in food preparation of your "Granny." Why? The "makins" are simply *not there*.

Do not be choosy. Pick up any food item in a supermarket and read the fine print on the package. Amazing. You will need the help of a chemist's dictionary to get an inkling of what the package contains. Here are a couple of tips. A loaf of bread that retails for a dollar fifty to three dollars contains only three cents worth of a farm commodity called wheat. The remainder is make believe. A large box of common cornflakes costs a bit less than four dollars. The fine print includes the word corn, another worldwide commodity, along with a multitude of other ingredients. These include a generous slug of chemicals with the well-accepted knowledge that the sealed package with advertising on all six sides costs the manufacturer more than the contents. Swallow that for breakfast, if you please. This is duplicated by many other staple food items. They are inspected and certified to be pure. Thank goodness.

What, then, is the problem? Where along this food train did we lose "Granny" with her succulent cuisine? It is in the basic makings. Chicken was selected as an example. It is universally acceptable wherever mentioned or used for food. It is certainly a primary item in our food chain. It is a perfect example.

Do you know how a dressed chicken, as offered for your approval in a supermarket, is produced? The only guidelines he *must* adhere to are the laws of nature. He should be tender, for he is only a few weeks out of the egg. He is fed and raised in an air conditioned battery brooder with his feet never once having the opportunity to scratch the terra firma. It is a steady path to slaughter as soon as the egg yolk remaining in the shell is consumed. He is fed objectively with the end goal in sight at all times, depending on the size that they wish him to reach before electrocution. This is an exercise in killing that does not always allow the victim to bleed out before blood congeals about the bones. This accounts for the dark portions of otherwise edible meat in packages of chicken you buy.

This young chicken is fed a progressive ration through self feeders from chick starter, grower and finisher. He eats roughly two and one quarter pounds of the chemical impregnated ration to make a pound of chicken. They keep squeezing down the amount of feed. The analysis can be changed as required and is watched closely by the United States Department of Agriculture. The consumer can buy with the assurance that the ingredients in this chicken mash are laced with all the growth stimulants the law allows. This policy duplicates goals of many of our other basic food items, to lawfully make all that is possible from our virgin commodities.

The vast difference is in the flavor of foods, in-

*It was a very wet year without a pullet visible anywhere. Will the market for fryers, eggs, and baby chicks be flooded out too by demand over quality?*

courtesy of The Flint Public Library

cluding chicken, when compared to what our Grannies used to make. Modern cooks cannot be blamed. It is the basic ingredients that they have to work with—the bird never had a decent crop full of food and grit in his life. The chicken Granny got to cook lived under far different circumstances. It would be a cockerel under six months old who was allowed free range of the premises and certainly had sexual experiences with the young pullets of the flock. This could

*This young Plymouth Rock possessed everything to make Granny's chicken dinner a feast. Notice the small spurs—he is young.*

change the flavor of his carcass somewhat, as it does to a boar, buck sheep or beef bull. This is an unknown and unresearched factor, but very possible. This young rooster has the range of the steading, scratching and picking up nutrients as needed to balance his diet. He would eat particular small stones for his gizzard to grind up insects, weed seeds, and kernels of wheat, barley and corn. He is therefore self made from his own selective feeding.

In the back of the house was always a pile of firewood or a woodshed full of fuel for the kitchen range. In the morning, after dishes, Granny would reach up and remove her wire chicken catcher from its hook, go to the corncrib and select an ear of corn that would shell easily. She would throw out a handful and the chickens would come rushing to her, unaware of her ulterior motive. After close observation, she would select a matured cockerel with a fully developed set of feathers that should be free from pesky pinfeathers. She used the hook to pull him toward her. In the second act in his supreme sacrifice she wrapped him in her apron with only his beautiful red head and comb visible. Other chickens took no heed. It was just a short walk to the block of wood behind the woodshed, and in the block of wood was stuck her trusty hatchet. Granny seized this prime young cockerel by the legs while placing his head just off the block with his neck stretched slightly. One clip and his head was separated from his body, which went to flopping about on the ground until he was fully bled out, as nature intended. By that time she came off the back porch with the large teakettle spouting steam. A scalding pail was brought forth and everyone within shouting distance was invited to help pick the chicken. It would be kind of a family bee with joking about whose turn it was to get this wishbone. The bird was placed in cold water, pumped from the northeast corner of the well, to separate the carcass from the body heat. There was no refrigeration of any description. After this cooling he was singed, washed good with homemade soap and water, and drawn.

He was put to cooking almost immediately. He weighed about seven pounds alive and was a bit too large for frying. Granny was in charge here. The chicken could be roasted and stuffed with dressing made from homemade bread or cut up, parboiled, fried and served with hot biscuits swimming in bowls of hot chicken gravy. With that method of preparation, dessert would be hot biscuits with home-churned butter and maple syrup.

Talk about a tasty chicken dinner. He was king for a day after being allowed to simmer and brown down on the kitchen range. They don't come that way anymore. The chicken today, in spite of all the concoctions they add, is much like chewing on a basswood stump. It is not the fault of the cook, restaurateur, or your imported chef, it is the adulterated basic makings. Chicken is not chicken any longer. It is a bundle of chemicals tucked under feathers.

That is why it can be truthfully stated that generations already here and generations unborn will never have the thrill of enjoying honest-to-God food. Chicken is only *one* example. These are the facts that cover our poultry and the entire food chain. I do not intend to pick on chicken. I use it only to provide a positive example, especially for those consumers who wonder why they cannot buy a good tasting chicken anymore. This goes for most meat. There is only one way to beat this commercialized racket in which you are a sucker. Raise your own or contract with a producer for your supply and store it in your own freezer. A Ralph Nader for our food supply is needed.

Commodities are beginning to embark on the same itinerary. If in doubt of any of these statements, pick up something you eat every day, read the list of contents that are published as required by law. Try a loaf of bread for instance. Many of the items listed will be in legal and scientific terms. Don't give up. Run the items down. You will be surprised and enlightened by the unneeded and often detrimental elements you are consuming without a serious thought about current or long-term effects. Yes, many of these unneeded, unwanted and detrimental chemicals that are being consumed daily have holdover tendencies. They are even capable of carrying on to the next generation.

Antibiotics are a class by themselves that inhibit growth and destroy bacteria. Penicillin is one of those antibiotics that builds up in a person. When help is needed to fight infection, it is ineffective because one unconsciously builds up an immunity. How? By consuming quantities of meat and foods containing streptomycin and other chemicals. When needed they are not effective. Quickly, it becomes a deathly situation.

Another group of compounded chemicals is capable of controlling heart action. These are used to increase food consumption, thus producing a marketable carcass in less time with fewer rations. Manufacturers of feeds containing these miracle chemicals are careful not to mention improvement in **quality of flavor**, because they are **nonexistent**. This subject needs deeper research that could reveal inconsistency and even fraud at the expense of the unsuspecting public. The consumer.

In closing this humorous and often serious publication, it is fortunate that this life has been given to me to spend now. It coincides with the greatest changes in our diet. Sad to say, they have not been for the best. This anti-nature movement must be reversed. It could control earth's population and provide room for "Granny's Luscious Cuisine." I accept the challenge. It has been my pleasure to tantalize you, my devoted reader, with humorous "Fowl Tales" used to introduce you to some simple truths that have developed throughout our food chain.

After these pages have been turned there remains the age old question, "What came first, the chicken or the egg?" Perhaps this image of a beautiful baby chick will help you to personally decide.

Stan Perkins

courtesy of U.S.D.A.